All About Me
Ryanne
Underhill

Dedications

We lovingly dedicate this book to Tyler and Justin...
and to all who choose to "see" from the inside out.
—HEIDI COLE AND NANCY VOGL

My book is dedicated to children everywhere.
It is up to us to show the way to a peaceful world.
—TYLER

I dedicate this book to my grandmother, Mildred Purnell.
Though she passed many years ago, she remains the kindest,
most gentle person I have ever known.
I love you Grandmom.
—GERALD PURNELL

Am I a Color Too?

Written by

Heidi Cole and Nancy Vogl

Illustrated by Gerald Purnell

ILLUMINATION Arts

BELLEVUE, WASHINGTON

People call my dad Black,
Like the dark night sky.

They say my mom is White,
Like the clouds way up high.

My mom and dad are different,
Yet very much the same.

They have smiles on their faces
And share the same last name.

A part of each of them
Is deep inside of me,

In my heart, in my soul,
In ways I've learned to see.

My dad,
  my mom,
    and me...
Black,
  White, and...
    am I a color too?

I think I'm just a person,
A person just like you.

When I'm in a busy crowd,
I see people from many places,

A brightly colored rainbow,
Of many different faces.

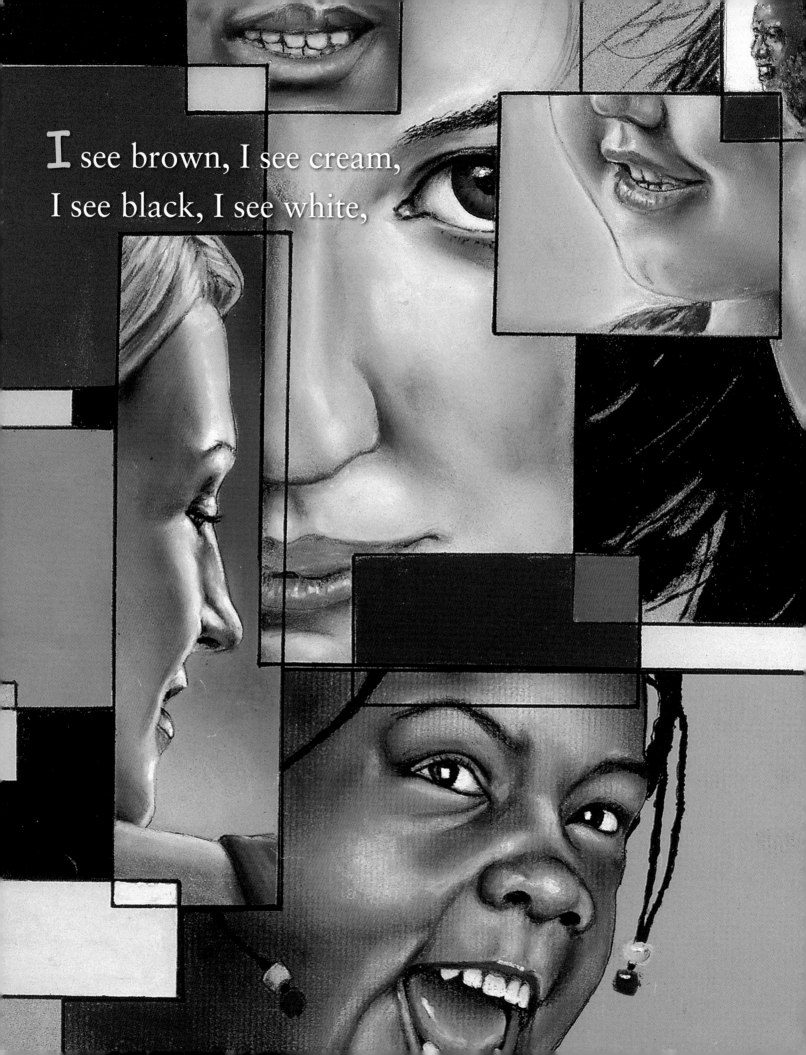

I see brown, I see cream,
I see black, I see white,

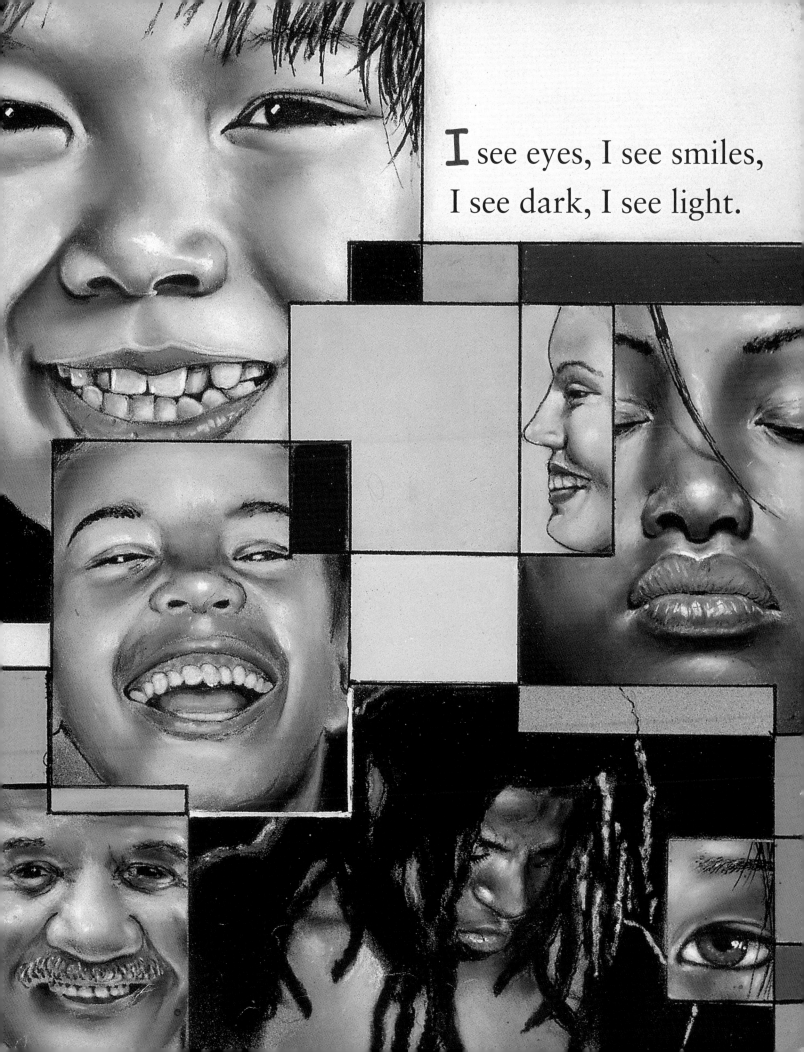

I see eyes, I see smiles,
I see dark, I see light.

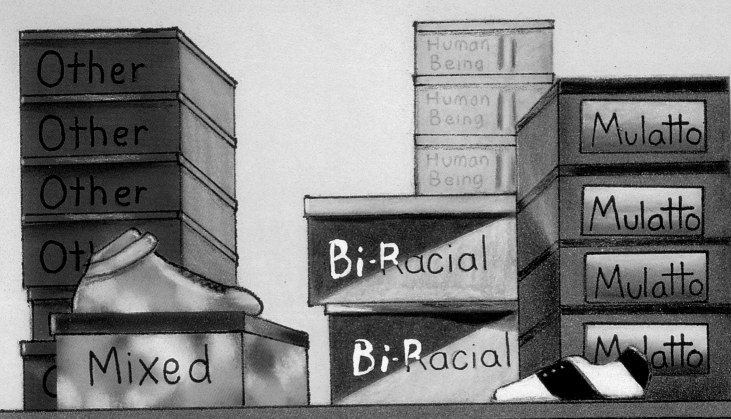

I'd like to find a word
That fits me like a shoe.

That's why I sometimes wonder
am I a color too?

When I think of all the people,
All those faces in my sight,

If people are really colors,
They must be more than
Black or White.

Because...

People see in every color
The beauty of each new day.

People smile in every color
And their troubles fade away.

People dance in every color.
To the music in their hearts.

People sing in every color.
Songs of joy with many parts.

People think in every color,
Not just in black and white.

People dream in every color,
And their world is filled with light.

People feel in every color.
We all hunger to be free.

People love in every color.
What a gift to you and me!

I am a Human Being,
Not a color, not a word.

I have my hopes and dreams
And a voice that will be heard.

My dad, my mom, and me,
Black, White, and…

am I a color too?

No, my name is Tyler.
I'm a person just like you.

Publishing Company, Inc.

P.O. Box 1865, Bellevue, WA 98009

Tel: 425-644-7185 • Fax: 425-644-9274

888-210-8216 (orders only)

liteinfo@illumin.com • www.illumin.com

Library of Congress Cataloging-in-Publication Data

Cole, Heidi, 1976-
   Am I a color too? / written by Heidi Cole and Nancy Vogl ; illustrated
by Gerald Purnell.
      p. cm.
   Summary: A young boy whose father is called Black and whose mother
is called White wonders if he is a color, too, even as he observes that
people around him dream, feel, sing, smile, and dance in every color.
   ISBN-13: 978-0-9740190-5-5 (hardcover : alk. paper)
   ISBN-10: 0-9740190-5-4 (hardcover : alk. paper)
   [1. Human skin color–Fiction.   2. Racially mixed people–Fiction.
3. Stories in rhyme.]   I. Vogl, Nancy.   II. Purnell, Gerald, ill.   III. Title.
PZ8.3.C67287Am 2005
[E]–dc22

                                                          2005015612

Published in the United States of America

Printed in Singapore by Tien Wah Press

Book Designer: Knockout Design, www.knockoutbooks.com

Front Cover Design: Murrah and Company, Kirkland, WA

Illumination Arts Publishing Company, Inc.

is a member of Publisher's in Partnership.

replanting our nation's forests.

More inspiring picture books from Illumination Arts

LITTLE YELLOW PEAR TOMATOES
Demian Elainé Yumei/Nicole Tamarin, ISBN 0-9740190-2-X

Ponder the never-ending circle of life through the eyes of a young girl, who marvels at all the energy and collaboration it takes to grow yellow pear tomatoes.

SOMETHING SPECIAL
Terri Cohlene/Doug Keith, ISBN 0-9740190-1-1

A curious little frog finds a mysterious gift outside his home near the castle moat. It's *Something Special*...What can it be?

THE TREE
Dana Lyons/David Danioth, ISBN 0-9701907-1-9

An urgent call to preserve our fragile environment, *The Tree* reminds us that hope for a brighter future lies in our own hands.

YOUR FATHER FOREVER
Travis Griffith/Raquel Abreu, ISBN 0-9740190-3-8

A devoted father promises to nurture, guide, protect and respect his beloved children. This heartwarming poem transcends the boundaries of culture and time in expressing a parent's universal love.

TOO MANY MURKLES
Heidi Charissa Schmidt/Mary Gregg Byrne, ISBN 0-9701907-7-8

Each spring the people of Summerville gather to prevent the dreaded Murkles from entering their village. Unfortunately, this year there are more of the strange, smelly creatures than ever.

WE SHARE ONE WORLD
Jane E. Hoffelt/Marty Husted, ISBN 0-9701907-8-6

Wherever we live — whether we work in the fields, the waterways, the mountains or the cities — all people and creatures share one world.

IN EVERY MOON THERE IS A FACE
Charles Mathes/Arlene Graston, ISBN 0-9701907-4-3

On this magical voyage of discovery and delight, children of all ages connect with their deepest creative selves.

A MOTHER'S PROMISE
Lisa Humphrey/David Danioth ISBN 0-9701907-9-4

A lifetime of sharing begins with the sacred vow a woman makes to her unborn child.

To view our whole collection visit us at www.illumin.com